Darcy and Gran Don't Like Babies

by JANE CUTLER
Illustrated by SUSANNAH RYAN

SCHOLASTIC INC.
New York Toronto London Auckland Sydney

ISBN 0-590-44588-X

12 11 10 9 8 7 6 5 4 3 2 1 9 5 6 7 8 9/9 0/0

Printed in the U.S.A. 09

Design by Claire B. Counihan

This artwork was drawn in charcoal and
painted with watercolor.

For Linda Allen,
agent and
friend.
—J.C.

For my sister Nancy
and our nephews William
and David.
—S.R.

Darcy didn't like the baby.

She didn't like his smell

and she didn't like his looks.

When someone asked her
how she liked the baby,
she told them.

Pretty soon, no one asked.
But that didn't stop Darcy.

"I don't like the baby," Darcy told her mother.

"But the baby is just like you were,
a long time ago," Darcy's mother said.

Darcy didn't care
about a long time ago.

"I don't like the baby," Darcy told her father.

"You'll like him better later on, when he can do more things," Darcy's father said.

Darcy didn't care about later on.

"I don't like the baby," Darcy told the doctor.

"You're not supposed to," said the doctor.

“I don’t like the baby,” Darcy told the neighbor.

“Of course you do,” the neighbor said.

"I don't like the baby," Darcy told her Gran.

"Me neither," said Darcy's Gran.

"I never did like babies."

“What don’t you like about them, Gran?” asked Darcy.
“I don’t much like their smell
and I don’t much like their looks,” said Gran.
“I don’t like all the work they make for everyone.
And besides, they get far too much attention.”

Darcy had nothing more to say.

"Want to go to the park, Darcy?" Gran asked.
"There will be a lot of babies in the park," Darcy warned.
"They won't be on the big swings," Gran said.
"They won't be on the tall slide," Darcy agreed.
"They won't be on the teeter-totter," Gran pointed out.
"They won't be on the jungle gym," Darcy remembered.
"They won't be in our way," said Gran. "Let's go."

Darcy and Gran put on their coats and their walking shoes. Gran put their gloves and hats in her backpack, in case the weather turned. Off they marched to the playground.
Gran walked fast. So did Darcy.
Gran looked straight ahead. So did Darcy.
Gran breathed deeply. So did Darcy.

When they got to the park,
they saw a lot of other people.
They saw a lot of babies.
The babies were in buggies.
The babies were in strollers.
The babies were in backpacks and frontpacks.
The babies were in mothers' arms.
The babies were on fathers' laps.
Some of the bigger babies
were in the sandbox, eating sand.
But not one baby was on the big swings.
Not one baby was on the tall slide.
Not one baby was on the teeter-totter.
Not one baby was on the jungle gym.
Not one baby was any place Darcy wanted to be.

"Babies all over the place," grumbled Gran.
"It's okay, Gran," Darcy said.
"They can't do anything we want to do.
That's the one thing I like about babies."

Darcy and Gran swung on the big swings

and slid down
the tall slide.

They rode on the teeter-totter

and climbed to the top of the jungle gym.

When the weather turned, they put on
their gloves and their hats and started home.

"Mom says the baby is
just like I was," Darcy said.
Gran thought.
"I believe that's true," she said.

"Dad says I'll like the baby better
later on," Darcy said.
Gran thought.
"I believe that's true," she said.

“The doctor says I’m not supposed to like the baby,” Darcy said.

Gran thought. “I believe the doctor means it’s okay if you don’t,” she said.

"Our neighbor says I *do* like the baby," Darcy said.

Gran thought.
"I believe your neighbor means *deep down*," she said.

"Do you think all the things
they say are right?" Darcy asked.
"I believe I do," said Gran.
"But what about you, Gran?"
"What about me, Darcy?"
"Are *you* going to like
the baby better later on?"

"I believe I will," said Gran.

"And is it okay if *you* don't like the baby now?"

"I believe it will have to be,"
Gran said. She smiled.

"And deep down do *you* like the baby, Gran?"
"I believe I *might*," allowed Gran.

“But you don’t think that baby is like *you* were when *you* were a baby, do you, Gran?”

“Oh, yes, Darcy,” Gran laughed, “I believe he is!”